BILLY AND THE MINI MONSTERS

Monsters at the Museum

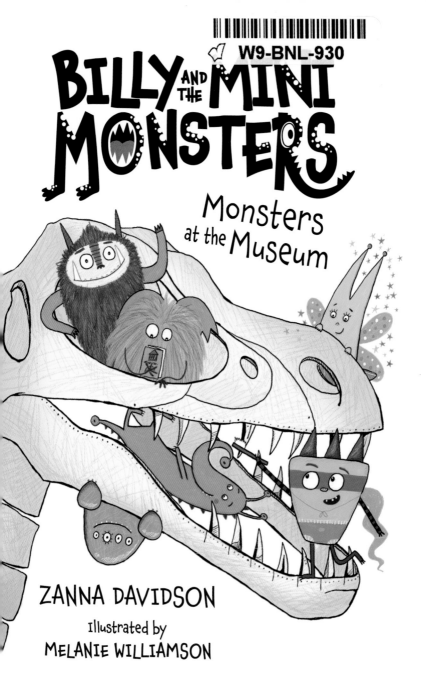

ZANNA DAVIDSON

Illustrated by
MELANIE WILLIAMSON

Reading consultant: Alison Kelly

Meet Billy...

Billy was just
an ordinary boy
living an ordinary
life, until
ONE NIGHT
he found
five
**MINI
MONSTERS**
in his sock drawer.

Gloop   Peep   Fang-Face   Captain Snott   Trumpet

Then he saved their lives, and
they swore never to leave him.

We give you
the Secret-Hairy-
Snot-Tooth Oath
of Devotion.

When he
moved to a
new house,
Billy found
ANOTHER
monster.

Hello. My
name's
Sparkle-
Boogey.

One thing was certain – Billy's
life would never be the same AGAIN...

Contents

Chapter 1
Invisible Billy

Billy was feeling nervous. He was getting ready for his FIRST EVER school trip, to a museum.

"That's exciting!" said Trumpet. "Why are you looking so sad?"

"Because I just started at my new school," Billy replied. "And I don't really know anyone yet."

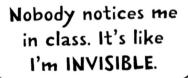

Nobody notices me in class. It's like I'm INVISIBLE.

"What about Ash from next door?" asked Gloop.

"He's in a different class!" said Billy. "No one will want to sit next to me, or be my partner."

"We'll come too," said the Mini Monsters. "We can sit next to you."

You can take us **REALLY SECRETLY** in your backpack.

We can see out of our special holes.

"Okay," said Billy, getting excited. "You can come if you promise not to make any trouble."

We promise!

Billy looked at the map of the museum. "Miss Potts, our teacher, said the museum's full of amazing things, like dinosaurs and creepy-crawlies and mummies."

MAP OF T

Gems

ELEVATOR

Creepy-crawlies

Dinosaurs

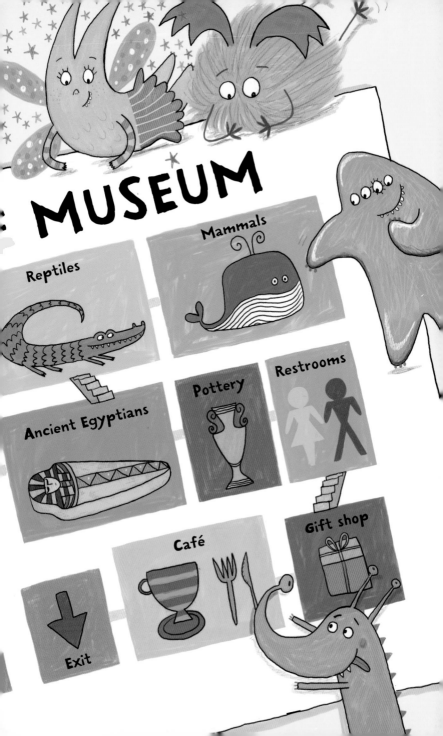

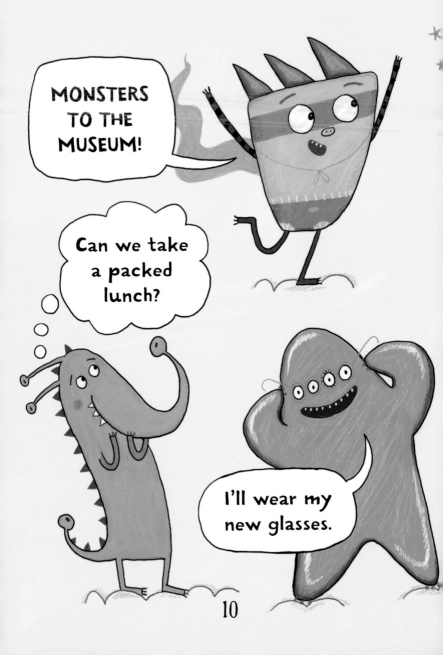

13

15

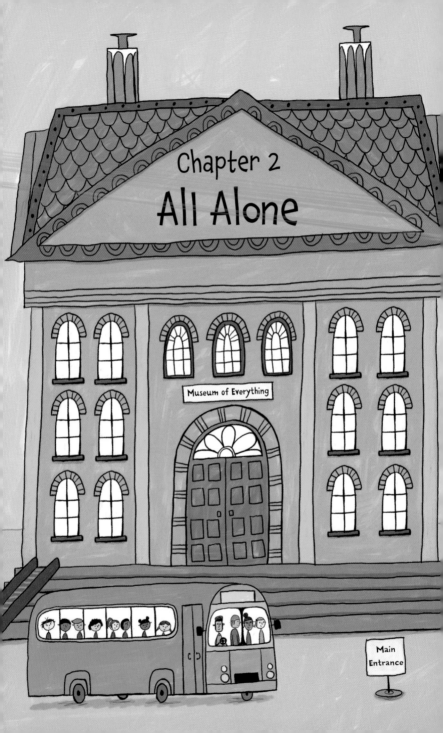

The bus pulled up outside the museum. "Wow!" said Billy.

It was HUGE.

"Everyone off the bus," said Billy's teacher, Miss Potts. "I want you all to line up and hold hands."

It's just like I thought. No one wants to be my partner.

"Now," said Miss Potts, once they were inside. "We're going to go around the museum in pairs and do a quiz."

Does everyone have a partner?

Billy raised his hand.

I don't have a partner.

Oh, you had better join in to make a three.

Billy looked at the other children. They all looked very happy in their pairs.

Miss Potts handed out the quiz sheets. "There'll be a **prize** for the winning team," she said.

"I really hope I win," thought Billy. "Then maybe people will notice me."

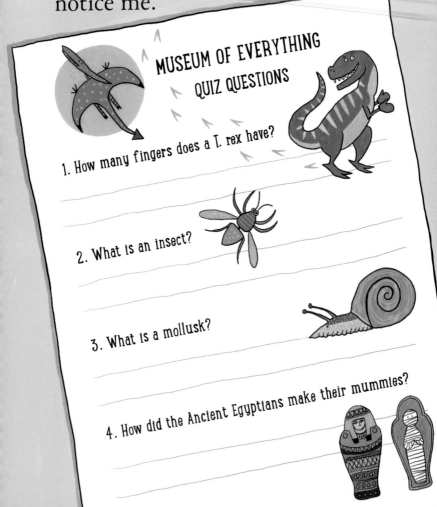

MUSEUM OF EVERYTHING
QUIZ QUESTIONS

1. How many fingers does a T. rex have?

2. What is an insect?

3. What is a mollusk?

4. How did the Ancient Egyptians make their mummies?

The questions looked really hard. Billy decided it was time to ask the Mini Monsters for help.

He opened up his bag.

But to his horror he saw that his bag was...

completely empty!

23

24

25

Chapter 3

Mommy Dinosaur

"First stop, the dinosaurs!" said Miss Potts.

Billy tried his hardest NOT to think about the Mini Monsters as he followed the line of children.

This way!

But he couldn't help thinking about what might be happening to them. What if they were…

…found and turned into an exhibit?

Or trapped in the museum ALL NIGHT?

Or lost in the big city?

"Here we are at the triceratops," said Miss Potts. "You can see the three horns on its head."

ROAR!

"Miss Potts! Miss Potts!" cried Billy's class. "The triceratops roared!"

"So it did!" said Miss Potts, jumping back in surprise.

Billy was sure he saw a flash of purple fur.

"And this is a velociraptor,"
Miss Potts went on, as they moved
onto the walkway. "They were
very vicious creatures."

"ROAR!" went
the velociraptor.

ROAR!

"M-m-my goodness," said Miss Potts. "What amazing sound effects."

This time, Billy definitely saw a flash of purple fur.

"And finally," said Miss Potts. "The T. rex skeleton."

Billy groaned. He could see Fang-Face, hiding behind one of the T. rex's ENORMOUS teeth.

As the other children moved on, Fang-Face began jumping up and down in excitement.

I've found my mommy!

She's scary just like me!

The more Fang-Face jumped, the more the skeleton wobbled.

Just then, one of the girls in Billy's class looked back. "The T. rex!" she cried. "It's moving.

It looks like it's... **alive!**"

"Nonsense," said Miss Potts.
Then she turned around.

Billy rushed forwards, to try
to grab Fang-Face.

"Step away, Billy!" called Miss Potts. "It doesn't look safe!"

But Billy knew he had to get Fang-Face. "What are you doing? That's a dinosaur, not your mommy. It died millions of years ago."

Oh!

Fang-Face leaped onto Billy's hand. "One down, five to go..." Billy thought, as he slipped Fang-Face into his backpack.

"Come on, children," said Miss Potts, trying to hurry everyone along. "I think we've had enough of the dinosaurs."

Two of the children smiled at Billy. Billy smiled back.

He was starting to feel a little bit less invisible.

39

40

Chapter 4
Creepy-Crawlies

"Here we are at the creepy-crawlies," said Miss Potts. "No roaring here, thank goodness."

She led them down a long
hallway lined with glass boxes.

"This is a stag beetle," said Miss
Potts. "The male stag beetles fight
each other with their huge jaws."

"Oooh!" said everyone in the class.
Everyone, that is, except Billy.

Billy had spotted Gloop INSIDE the ant tank.

He tapped on the glass as quietly as he could. "Gloop!" he hissed.

What are you doing?

You have to get out of there!

"Miss Potts!" shouted a boy. "What's that blue thing in the ant cage?"

"It doesn't look very happy," said the boy. "Someone should get it out."

"It's got four eyes!" said a girl. "And…are those glasses?"

"Look, Miss Potts!"
everyone shouted.
"Look!"
"I'll get it out!" cried Billy. He
plunged his arm into the ant tank.

Billy tried to ignore the ants **SCUTTLING** over his skin. At last, his fingers closed around Gloop. Then Miss Potts came running over.

You're not supposed to put your arm in there.

Everyone looked at Billy.
"Where *is* the blue thing?"

"**Oh!**" said Billy,
slipping Gloop
into his backpack.
"It…ran off."

"I don't like this place,"
muttered Miss Potts.
"First roaring
dinosaurs…

…and now strange
blue slimy things.

Move along, children…"

48

"Yes please," said Billy.

As they walked to the next exhibit, Billy smiled.

"**WOW**," he thought. "I think I'm starting to make friends."

THEN THE BODY WAS FILLED WITH STUFFING.

Yikes.

THE BODY WAS WRAPPED IN LINEN.

Amazing!

52

53

Chapter 5
Mommies & Mommies

Billy followed Miss Potts to the
Ancient Egyptian hall. He still had
FOUR Mini Monsters to find.

"Do you know where the others are?" he whispered to Fang-Face and Gloop.

"They're probably looking for their mommies," said Gloop. "You said we'd see mommies at the museum."

I said **MUMMMIES** not **MOMMIES!**

Ohhh!

"Here we have an amazing mummy," Miss Potts was saying.

This one is over **2,000** years old.

"And there are two really tiny mummies," said one of the girls. "Aren't they sweet."

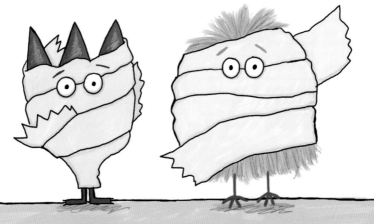

Billy's heart sank.

There, in front of everyone, were Peep and Captain Snott…

mummified!

"They're not real," said Miss Potts. "It looks like someone's made mummies of their toys."

Miss Potts **picked** up Peep. And then…

Peep sneezed.

Miss Potts screamed.

The class screamed too.

Everyone started running
this way and that.

Aaargh!

It's a HAUNTED
MUSEUM!

While no one was watching, Billy grabbed Peep and Captain Snott and put them in his bag.

I need a **cup** of **coffee!**

Miss Potts looked like she might faint. "Can I help?" asked Billy.

61

62

63

Chapter 6
Friends at Last

Billy led Miss Potts and the rest of the class to the café so they could all calm down.

Here's a cup of coffee to make you feel better.

"Thank you, Billy," said Miss Potts, sitting down.

What a good boy you are.

Billy felt a little guilty, seeing as it was **HIS** Mini Monsters that had scared Miss Potts. But he couldn't really tell her that.

65

"Now," Miss Potts said to the class, after she'd had her cup of coffee, "I'd like you to fill in your quiz sheets."

Oh no! I can't answer **ANY** of these.

Billy looked at the questions in **despair**.

He'd been too busy worrying about the **MINI MONSTERS** to look for the answers.

"Hey, Billy!" called Ella. "Come and sit with us."

"I'm not sure I'll be very good at the quiz," said Billy. But then he heard a whisper in his ear.

Billy was able to help answer

EVERY SINGLE

question.

But as soon as they'd handed in their quiz sheets, Miss Potts said, "Come on, everyone, time to go."

"Uh oh!" thought Billy. He'd been so excited about making friends, he'd forgotten about Trumpet and Sparkle-Boogey.

Then he heard a cry from the front of the café. "Look!" shouted a man. "There's a mouse here eating some cheese. And a giant pink fly."

As Billy **rushed** towards the cheese, Miss Potts let out another scream. "**A MOUSE? I HATE MICE!**"

Billy **picked** up Trumpet
and Sparkle-Boogey…

ran
past the
screaming
customers…

and **raced**
after his
classmates.

"Thank you for your help
today," Billy whispered to the Mini
Monsters. "Because of you I finished
the quiz AND made new friends."

"But we made so **much** trouble," said Peep.

"For once," said Billy, grinning, "you made just the right kind of trouble."

And even though we didn't find our mommies, maybe we don't need them.

YOU can be our mommy!

When Billy got back on the bus, he found Ella and Stan sitting on the back row.

Come and sit with us!

Billy smiled and went over to join them.

"Now," said Miss Potts, when everyone was sitting down. "The winners of the quiz are...Stan, Ella and our new student, Billy!"

"And here's your prize," she went on, handing them a bag full of toys. There were plastic dinosaurs, mummies and creepy-crawlies.

"Wow," thought Billy. Then he had an idea. He whispered it to Ella and Stan, who nodded in agreement.

By the time
Billy sat down again,
he was grinning. This had
been the best school trip EVER.

All about the MINI MONSTERS

CAPTAIN SNOTT →

LIKES EATING: boogeys.

SPECIAL SKILL:
can glow in the dark.

SCARE
FACTOR:
5/10

← GLOOP

LIKES EATING: cake.

SPECIAL SKILL:
very stre-e-e-e-tchy.
Gloop can also swallow his own
eyeballs and make them reappear
on any part of his body.

SCARE
FACTOR:
4/10

FANG-FACE →

LIKES EATING:
socks, school ties, paper, or
anything that comes his way.

SPECIAL SKILL:
has massive fangs.

SCARE
FACTOR:
9/10

TRUMPET →

LIKES EATING: cheese.

SPECIAL SKILL:
amazingly powerful
cheese-powered toots.

SCARE FACTOR:
7/10

(taking into
account his toots)

PEEP

LIKES EATING: very small flies.

SPECIAL SKILL: can fly (but
not very far, or very well).

SCARE FACTOR:
0/10 (unless you're afraid of
small hairy things)

SPARKLE-BOOGEY →

LIKES EATING:
glitter and boogeys.

SPECIAL SKILL:
can shoot out
clouds of glitter.

SCARE FACTOR:
5/10 (if you're scared of
pink sparkly glitter)

MUSEUM OF EVERYTHING
QUIZ ANSWERS from page 20

1. How many fingers does a T. rex have? Two on each hand.

2. What is an insect? An insect is a small animal with six legs and a body that has three separate parts. Many insects also have wings.

3. What is a mollusk? A mollusk is a creature with a soft body and no backbone, usually protected by a shell.

4. How did the Ancient Egyptians make their mummies? The body was first washed. Then the internal organs were removed (apart from the heart). The body was then filled with stuffing and dried out. Once dried, the body was wrapped in linen and oils and covered in a shroud, before being placed in a stone or wooden container.

Series editor: Becky Walker
Designed by Brenda Cole
Cover design by Hannah Cobley
Digital manipulation by John Russell

First published in 2018 by Usborne Publishing Ltd., Usborne House, 83-85 Saffron Hill, London EC1N 8RT, England. www.usborne.com
Copyright © 2018 Usborne Publishing Ltd. AE